CALLY & JIMMY

TWINTASTIC

CALLY & JIMMY

TWINTASTIC

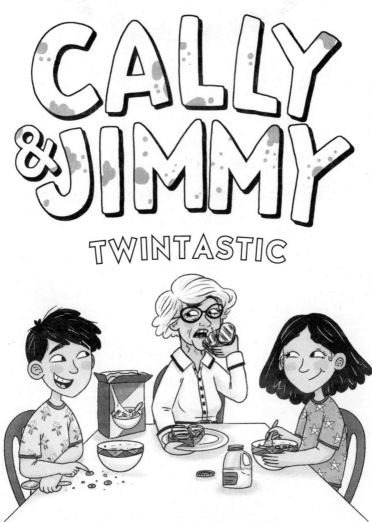

ZOE ANTONIADES

ILLUSTRATED BY **KATIE KEAR**

ANDERSEN PRESS

For Dominic

First published in 2021 by
Andersen Press Limited
20 Vauxhall Bridge Road
London SW1V 2SA
www.andersenpress.co.uk

2 4 6 8 10 9 7 5 3 1

British Library Cataloguing in Publication Data available.

ISBN 978 1 83913 016 8

MIX
Paper from
responsible sources
FSC   FSC® C012700

Printed and bound in Great Britain by Clays Ltd, Elcograf S.p.A.

TTT TWINS

TRICK-OR-TREAT TWINS

TRACKTASTIC TWINS

TRAVELLING TWINS

TTT
TWINS

Hi, I'm Cally and this is my twin Jimmy. There are three things you need to know about him: one, he's the most-annoying-brother-in-the-whole-wide-world. Two, sometimes he can't help being annoying because he's got ADHD, which means he finds it hard to concentrate and he usually acts before he thinks. And three, even though he's annoying, I'm pretty sure he's Mum and Yiayia's favourite.

Yiaiyia's our Greek granny from Cyprus. She moved in to help look after us when Mum and Dad split up. It's sad that we can't live with

3

Dad too but we still stay with him every other weekend and he always comes to any special events that we are going on. I think if Dad was around more, things would be a bit fairer cos I reckon I'm Dad's favourite. We're both good at maths and like marmalade and marmite sandwiches. But now it's just Mum and Yiayia, and when it comes to getting attention and your own way, Jimmy pretty much gets it all if you ask me. Except nobody ever does ask me, cos it's always all about Jimmy in *our* house.

Jimmy's latest obsession is collecting Mega Mash Machines cards. It's one pound for a pack of seven. He's already spent his birthday money on them. Such a rip off. Seven silly cards with pictures of robots that are meant to smash each other up because of their special attachments and turbo-boost fuel points.

Jimmy's got a stack of them so big that when he stuffs them in his trouser pockets it makes him walk funny – like he's some sort of robot himself. To be fair, practically everyone else at school is mad about them too – even my best friend Aisha. I can't understand it myself. But if they want to get all tragic swapping and competing with each other over who's got the rarest card, then that's their problem.

Our teacher, Mrs Wright, isn't a fan of the cards either. 'It'll all end in tears,' she keeps saying. And as for Miss Loretta, Jimmy's teaching assistant, she's been having a nightmare trying to stop Jimmy from getting distracted by them in class. It's hard enough trying to get him to concentrate as it is. I bet Miss Loretta wishes she had a Mega Mash Machine to deal with Jimmy sometimes. They have an arrangement where she looks after his cards during lessons and he gets to take them out at playtimes only. Mrs Wright has a massive

 5

confiscated stash on her desk cos no one is allowed them in class. So loads of the kids keep theirs hidden in their bags and jackets on the pegs at the back of the classroom.

I feel sorry for Yiayia the most, because on our way to school, we can't go past the shops without the usual Mega Mash Machines nonsense. Last week was no different.

'Please, Yiayia. Please can we get just one pack? Please,' Jimmy said, tugging on her shawl.

We? Not as if there's ever anything in it for me or Yiayia.

'No, no. No today, Jimmy mou. Let's be just to go to school,' said Yiayia.

'*Pleeeeeease*. Just one pack. I'm trying to get the Techtronic Titan Trasher.'

I rolled my eyes. 'What's so special about a stupid Trashy Titan anyway?'

Jimmy looked at me as if I'd just insulted God or something.

6

'What's so *special* about it?! The Techtronic Titan Trasher only happens to be like the rarest card in the whole wide world! I mean, it's the TTT, Cally, don't you even know *anything*? **Turbo Boost**: ten trillion. **Weapon**: the Claw AND the Shredder AND the Incinerator. **Material**: titanium – of course. **Time of Manufacture**: the Apocalypse. And it's GOLD!'

Most Mega Mash Machines cards are normal cardboard, but some have holographic, shiny borders in bronze or silver. The TTT is the only gold one – apparently. *Whoop-de-doo*!

'Please, please . . .'

Jimmy was now doing his full-on begging act, clasping his hands under his chin and gazing up at Yiayia with puppy-dog eyes. She was going to cave in as usual. I knew it.

'All right, Jimmy mou,' she said, scrabbling about in her handbag for her little purse and taking out a pound coin.

'Thanks, Yiayia. You're the bestest Yiayia timesed by ten trillion,' he said, giving her a massive hug.

'Just go and get your stupid cards then, and stop making us late for school,' I said.

'You want get something from shop too, Calista mou?' said Yiayia, sorting through the coins in her purse.

'No, it's OK, Yiayia. Thanks, though.'

Jimmy raced into the shop and was back out on the pavement in seconds, ripping open his Mega Mash Machines pack like a maniac.

'*Demon Demolisher* . . . got . . . *Critter Crusher* . . . got . . . *Herculean Hurricane* . . . got . . .'

'So, you've basically got all of them already. Great use of one pound,' I said.

'I can swap them at school though, can't I?' he said, flicking through the rest of the pack.

'I take it the famous TTT isn't there, then?'

Jimmy shook his head.

'Surprise, surprise! Now can we *please* just get to school. Some of us do actually want to do something with our brains, you know.'

'Nerd,' said Jimmy.

Yiayia stood between us, took each of us by the hand, and we walked the rest of the way to school like that.

When we arrived in the playground, I knew something important had happened, because instead of the kids hanging around near their classrooms where they're meant to line up when the bell goes, there was a massive bunch of people all crowding round Year Five.

We kissed Yiayia goodbye and raced over to see what was up. Pushing our way through the crowd, I realised it was actually my best friend Aisha who was at the centre of it all. She was clutching something tightly to her chest and looking a bit panicked as everyone scrambled over each other to get to her.

'Is it true?'

'Aisha's got the TTT!'

'No way!'

'For real?'

'The Techtronic Titan Trasher?!'

'Let's have a look! Let's have a look!'

'I'll swap ya!'

'I'll give you my whole complete collection for that one card, Aisha, what do you say?'

My poor friend Aisha. She looked terrified. I had to do something. 'Mrs Wright's coming! Mrs Wright's coming!' I said.

And then everyone was whispering, 'Mrs Wright's coming! Mrs Wright's coming!' and scattering back to their classes and getting into line and acting as if everything was all normal, cos we all knew what Mrs Wright would do if she saw that card and the fuss it was causing. She'd confiscate it, of course. And then no one would even get the chance to try and do a swap.

So we all lined up as good as gold. Even Jimmy. And he's rubbish at lining up. He has his own special lining up place at the front because he always pushes everyone accidentally-on-purpose. Mrs Wright looked a bit suspicious – especially as we'd all managed our line up order so perfectly before the bell had even gone. Aisha tucked the super-rare card into the inside pocket of her jacket. Mrs Wright would never know.

But *we* all did. I could feel the news rising in the air and buzzing through the line. Like some sort of secret raging hunger that everyone had

 12

for that card. And no one more so than Jimmy, cos even though he was at the front of the line with his back to me, and I couldn't see his face, I could just tell, that he, my twin Jimmy, wanted that card the most.

★

When it was playtime, Aisha left her jacket on the pegs in class with the TTT safely hidden away in it. Wise move. At least she wouldn't get ambushed again.

But even though she didn't have the card with her, it didn't stop everyone coming up and pestering her anyway. *So* annoying. We were sitting on the benches and I was doing Aisha's hair. Well I was trying to, if people would just leave us alone. Aisha has the longest, silkiest hair ever. Mine's all bushy and sticky-outy and not long at all. So Aisha lets me do plaits on hers.

Jimmy was the first to come bouncing over:

 13

'Hey, Aisha, show me the TTT. I just want to have a look.'

'Go away, Jimmy,' we both said at the same time. We're besties, so that often happens.

Then came Mitch Moran.

'Is it true, Aisha? Have you really got the TTT? What's it like? What's it like?'

'I haven't got it,' said Aisha. ' . . . Well, I have, but not here, right now,' she explained.

Next was Candice Solomon.

She's our friend at least, so Aisha told her and me all about the moment when she discovered she'd got the TTT. She'd bought the pack from the corner shop yesterday on her way home from school.

'Wow!' said Candice in awe. 'I can't believe it was right there in that shop. Like literally down our street. Any one of us could have got that. You're well lucky, Aisha.' Candice was being a good sport. I could tell she was jealous, but at least she had some dignity. Unlike Jimmy, who was bounding across the playground to bother us – again!

'Pleeeeeeeaaaase, can I just have a little look?'

'We said go away, Jimmy!'

Then Jackson Boyle came over. 'I'll give you ten pounds for it,' he said.

'You haven't got ten pounds, Jackson,' I said. I feel sorry for Jackson sometimes. His parents never come to Sports Days or the Christmas plays or anything like that.

He hangs around after school with his big cousin, Dermot, all the time. Dermot's a teenager, and quite scary. And he doesn't wear his trousers properly – he has them a bit down so you can see his pants – and not even by accident.

Jackson put his hands in his pockets, hung his head and wandered off quietly.

And then Jimmy was back again, hopping from one foot to the other. 'I only want to see it. Come on, Aisha. It's not fair.'

'She hasn't even got it on her!' I yelled at him. 'She left it inside.'

Jimmy went running off. We didn't see him again for the rest of the playtime. Must have found someone else to annoy after that. At least it wasn't us.

When we got back into class, Aisha went straight to her jacket to have another look at the precious TTT. She slipped her hand into the inside pocket. And gasped. Then she turned her jacket inside out and shook it. Panic was written all over her face.

'What is it, Aisha?' I said.

'It's not there!' She looked like she might faint.

'Aisha Khan,' came Mrs Wright's voice from the other side of the classroom. 'What are you doing there in the coat area? Hurry up and sit down. We've got work to do.'

Aisha staggered over to the 'top table', where we sit next to each other. Her eyes had welled up.

'Don't worry,' I whispered. 'We'll find it.'

Aisha didn't reply. She just sat there, staring down at the desk in deep shock.

 17

Mrs Wright began the maths lesson. Maths is my and Aisha's favourite. I don't want to sound like a show-off but we're both pretty good at it and sometimes Mrs Wright has to get us worksheets from Year Six even though we're only in Year Five.

But today, Aisha wasn't answering a single question. She didn't put her hand up once. She wasn't even writing on her whiteboard. Great big tears started to drop onto the desk.

plop...
plop...
plop...

'Aisha?' said Mrs Wright. 'Is anything the matter?'

Aisha shook her head. She still couldn't speak.

'Aisha? This isn't like you. What's wrong?'

Aisha buried her head in her arms on the desk and started sobbing. I could see her shoulders going up and down. She was devastated.

Mrs Wright turned to me. 'Cally? Do you know what's upset Aisha?'

'Someone . . . someone's taken her TTT card!'

The entire class gasped in horror.

'Her TTT . . . ?' said Mrs Wright, looking a bit confused.

'It's the rarest Mega Mash Machines card ever. And Aisha had it,' explained Mitch Moran.

Mrs Wright put her hand to her forehead, like Mum does when she's got one of her

19

headaches, and she sighed a very deep sigh. 'Those . . . silly, *silly* cards,' she said.

The maths lesson was clearly not going to happen now, so she went on, 'OK, then, let's get to the bottom of this . . . So, when did the card go missing?'

Aisha took her head up off the desk. Her eyes were red raw and her face was all puffy. She still couldn't speak.

'It must have been at playtime, Miss,' I explained. 'Because she had it this morning and it was in her coat, but when we got back it wasn't there any more.'

'I see. So, someone must have been inside during break, then.' Mrs Wright frowned.

We're not meant to come in, unless we've got a special pass for Chess Club or Choir or something.

'Did anyone see anyone coming into the classroom?' Mrs Wright folded her arms and scanned the room for suspects.

20

Nina Wilinska raised her hand gingerly. 'Please, Miss. It was Jimmy. I saw him come back in through the door by the toilets.'

Jimmy glared at Nina. Everyone glared back at him. *Aisha* glared at me!

No way. It couldn't have been my twin Jimmy. Aisha, my best friend, would hate me for ever if it was.

'Jimmy, is this true?' said Mrs Wright.

'It wasn't *me* . . . it wasn't me . . .' he stammered. He'd gone bright red.

'Well, did you come inside at playtime, or not?'

'I . . . I . . . well . . . I *did*. But it . . . it was for my fruit. I'd left my snack behind. It wasn't to get Aisha's card . . .' Jimmy was looking all stressed out. 'I didn't do it . . .'

I believed him. He's my brother. And he might be the-most-annoying-brother-in-the-whole-wide-world, but he's not a liar. I know that. I had to believe him. The rest of the class didn't, though. *Especially* not Aisha. She looked up at Mrs Wright and said, 'Please, Miss, see if he's got it.'

'OK, Jimmy. Stand up and turn out your pockets,' said Mrs Wright.

'But . . . but . . . I didn't . . . I haven't . . .'

'Just, do it, Jimmy. Now. Please,' said Mrs Wright, trying her best to control her temper. She's one of those lovely teachers who hardly ever shouts or anything, but I could see even *she* was losing her patience now.

 22

Jimmy stood up, shaking. He emptied out his pockets. There was a bit of fluffy Blu Tack – he's always peeling it off the back of Mrs Wright's displays, so she wasn't too pleased to see that. But she didn't say anything because now it was all about the TTT. There was a small toy car and a handful of his own Mega Mash Machines cards which he'd managed to sneak away from Miss Loretta – *she* didn't look too pleased about that either. But no TTT card.

'Now let's have a look in your tray please, Jimmy. And, Miss Loretta, if you could search Jimmy's coat and book bag, thank you.'

Jimmy started to cry. 'I didn't . . . it wasn't . . .'

Still no TTT card.

'OK, sit down please, Jimmy,' said Mrs Wright. 'Don't worry, Aisha, we'll get to the bottom of this. But what was a sensible girl like you doing bringing such a thing into school? I said it would all end in tears.' Mrs Wright was shaking her head. She looked really fed up. She must have been, because she gave up trying to teach us in the fun way she normally does and gave us all a boring, easy maths paper and made us work in silence for the rest of the lesson.

When Mrs Wright wasn't looking, I whispered to Aisha, 'You didn't have to make them search him like that. You know how Jimmy gets upset so easily.'

'And *you* know how much he wanted that card,' she said.

'Aisha, practically *everyone* wants that stupid card. Why would it have to be Jimmy?'

'Cos he was inside at playtime, wasn't he?'

'But he was getting his fruit . . .'

'How do you know that though?'

24

'I just do. Jimmy's a lot of things, but he's not a thief.'

'Well you *would* stick up for him, because he's your twin.'

'And you're supposed to be my best friend. So I don't think it's very nice of you to be so horrible about my brother. Anyway, they've just gone through all his stuff, haven't they? Jimmy hasn't got your dumb card.'

Aisha shifted her chair away from me. It scraped the floor and caught Mrs Wright's attention. So we couldn't say anything else to each other. I didn't think we'd be speaking to each other after all that anyway.

★

When Yiayia came to pick us up from school, Jimmy burst into tears all over again, so he got all the attention and fuss and cuddles, even though I was the one who'd lost my best friend and was dying inside too.

It was Friday, at least, so we were going to Dad's for our every-other-weekend sleepover. But even that couldn't cheer us up. When Dad came to call for us, he said, 'Why the glum faces?'

Mum shook her head and said, 'It's a long story.'

Dad ruffled Jimmy's hair, tweaked my nose, took our bags and said, 'Best tell me all about it in the car, then.'

So we did. And by the time we'd arrived in Clapham, Dad had the full story.

'Thing is,' Dad said as we all piled out of the car. 'For every problem, there's a solution.'

'Not this time, Dad,' I said. 'This one's really bad.'

'Yeah,' agreed Jimmy. 'Really bad timesed by ten trillion.'

'Come on, now. What's happened to my *Twinvincibles*, hey? I'm sure we can sort this out somehow.'

'Not unless we can miraculously get Aisha her card back,' I said.

And then Jimmy started bouncing about. 'That's it! We'll get Aisha another card!'

'What are you on about? You know how rare those things are. What are we supposed to do? Buy every single pack of cards from every single shop? We're not millionaires, in case you hadn't realised.'

'Cyber Trader! We could see if there's one online. Dad? You've got an account, haven't you?'

Actually, that wasn't such a bad idea. Cyber Trader's this website where people buy and sell stuff. It's like an auction. People list something on the website, and you have to bid for it. Then, the person who's offered the highest price by the end-of-sale date, gets it.

'OK, then. Let's get inside and have some tea, then maybe we'll take a look,' said Dad. Dad's the best.

28

Dad made sausages, beans and chips. Jimmy ate it so quickly he got hiccups. 'Come on, Dad. Come on, Cally. We need to do this,' he said, jumping off his chair and grabbing Dad's laptop bag.

'OK, Jimmy. Calm down,' said Dad.

Calming down's not exactly Jimmy's thing. Dad might as well have asked him to sneeze with his eyes open.

So, we quickly cleared the table and huddled round the laptop. Dad got the internet up and went onto Cyber Trader.

'OK then, what are we searching for?' he said.

I'm surprised he needed to ask. Jimmy had been going on about the TTT card ever since Mega Mash Machines came into existence.

'Put in *Techtronic Titan Trasher*,' said Jimmy.

So Dad did. And when he hit the search button, three items came up. One of them was ripped – so that was no good. 'And it's still got bids of up to twenty-nine pounds ninety-nine!' Dad choked. 'I dread to think what an undamaged one would go for.'

'And that one's clearly a fake,' said Jimmy, pointing at the second picture. 'The gold is normal-like. The real proper actual ones have holograms.'

Dad scrolled down to the third one and clicked on it so we could see the whole page. There it was. The real thing. An actual TTT card.

 30

TECHTRONIC TITAN TRASHER

⚡ TURBO BOOST-
10,000,000,000,000

WEAPONS: THE CLAW, THE SHREDDER, THE INCINERATOR
MATERIAL: TITANIUM TIME OF MANUFACTURE: THE APOCALYPSE

Jimmy sprang up and started leaping around the room and jumping on the sofa. 'Let's get it for Aisha! Let's get it for Aisha!'

'Hold on a second,' said Dad.

'Let's see what it's going for . . . hmmm . . . the bids are already up to a hundred pounds and there's still five more days of the sale to go . . . I can't afford that.'

Jimmy came rushing back up to the screen. 'But we have to. Click on *Bid,* Dad. Click on *Bid*. Pleeeeease! You'll never have to get me a Christmas present or a birthday present ever again . . . or maybe not ever again . . . but for the next ten years at least . . .' Jimmy only said that cos he knew Dad would never not buy him any presents.

 31

'Look, we'll click on *Watch* and keep an eye on it for now, how about that?' Dad suggested. He could tell Jimmy was close to having a meltdown.

'Go on, then. Do that, then. Do that, then,' said Jimmy.

So that's what we did. And when we clicked *Watch*, another screen came up saying: *Thank you for registering your interest with Der-Boy.*

Anyone who's selling anything on Cyber Trader has a nickname and Der-Boy was the one with the TTT card.

'Ha! Ha! Der-Boy!' squealed Jimmy. 'Der-Boy, Der-Boy!'

But I wasn't laughing. Not only because Jimmy was being ridiculous as usual, but because there was something else. Something about his nickname.

'Let's see his profile, Dad. Where does he live?'

'Well it already says here, underneath the

price, that he's based in West London,' said Dad. 'Doesn't give an exact location though.'

'But, click on *Seller information*. Let's see if there's a photo of him,' I said.

So Dad did. And there it was. Der-Boy's ugly mug. Staring out at us from the Cyber Trader screen. It *was* him!'

'Der-Boy!' I gasped.

'What about him, Cally?' Dad looked to me for an explanation.

'There's this boy in our class. Jackson Boyle. He's got a scary cousin called Dermot. Dermot Boyle. Der-Boy. See? It's definitely him! I think Jackson must have stolen the card from Aisha and given it to his big cousin, to impress him or something.'

Jimmy froze on the spot. Actually standing still for once. His mouth was wide open. His eyes were popping out of his head. 'Cally, you're a total genius. That's exactly what must have happened. And now I think about it, I swear I saw Jackson go past me when I was on my way out from getting my fruit at playtime. We have to tell Aisha! NOW!'

Dad held out his hands and said, 'Hold on,

 34

hold on. This is a bit delicate. We can't just go accusing people. I think we need to speak with the school first. Let them handle this. They'll need to talk to Jackson and his parents and so on.'

I was desperate to make things up with Aisha. I didn't want to have to go through the whole weekend until school sorted things out. But Dad was right. This was a bit tricky and probably something the grown-ups needed to deal with.

'But what if someone else buys it?' said Jimmy.

'The end-of-sale date isn't until Tuesday so that card's not going anywhere for now. Try not to worry. Tell you what, I'll email the school. I'll send them a screenshot and a link to the site too. How about that? I'm sure they'll get onto it first thing on Monday morning,' said Dad.

'Jackson's going to be in soooooooooo much trouble,' said Jimmy.

'Now, now,' said Dad. 'Best not to make too big a thing of it. I'm sure Jackson just made a silly mistake. I bet he's already feeling very bad about things too.'

But this *was* a big thing. It would be all round school next week for sure. Poor Jackson. If he hadn't stolen from Aisha and practically destroyed my friendship with her, I might almost have felt sorry for him too.

★

On Monday morning, Jimmy was under strict instructions to keep quiet about everything and anything to do with the Mega Mash Machines situation until the school had dealt with it. It would be bad if rumours started spreading and Jackson knew he'd been found out before the teachers had talked to him. He might try to change the story. He might get his cousin to destroy the TTT. He might run away (he has done that before – he only got as far as hiding behind the PE equipment shed, but still). Anything could happen.

Mum had given Yiayia five pounds to bribe Jimmy with. If he could just control himself that morning and keep quiet, he'd be allowed to get five packs of Mega Mash Machines cards on the way home from school. Five pounds. They were spoiling Jimmy again. But then, it was a massive deal for Jimmy. Jimmy doesn't do 'control' very well.

When we arrived at school, Aisha still wasn't talking to me. I tried not to blame her. Jimmy had been inside at playtime when her card went missing and everyone else had thought it was him too. But everything would soon be all right again, now I'd worked out who the real thief was. Aisha just didn't know it yet. Keeping it a secret until the grown-ups had fixed things made me want to burst, I could only imagine what it must have been like for Jimmy.

As Mrs Wright began taking the register, there was a knock at the door. It was Mr Matthews, the headteacher. Mrs Wright nodded as he entered. It seemed she was expecting him. Mr Matthews pointed at Jackson Boyle and summoned him with his finger. Jackson went bright red. He slowly got up and, hanging his head, followed the headteacher out of the classroom.

Everyone started whispering to the person next to them. 'Jackson's in trouble, Jackson's in trouble,' and, 'What d'you think he's done?'

Jimmy sits at his own table by Mrs Wright's desk with Miss Loretta next to him, and even though I could only see the back of his head, I could tell he was trying super hard to keep everything inside. Miss Loretta put her hand on his shoulder and patted him on the back. It was hard for me too, but I managed to stay quiet, even though I just wanted to scream, 'It wasn't even Jimmy! It was Jackson!'

'Now, now, everybody,' said Mrs Wright. 'Can we all just pipe down so that we can finish the register and get to assembly?'

Afterwards, when we were filing down the corridor towards the hall, Mr Matthews came and got me and Aisha and Jimmy too! We followed Mr Matthews in silence. Behind us I could hear the rest of the class exploding into whispers again and Mrs Wright doing her best to shush everyone.

When Mr Matthews opened the door to his office, we could see Jackson sitting at the big, round desk that the staff use for important meetings. We couldn't see his face because his head was still hung so low. He was sitting in total silence. I mean, Jackson's one of the quiet boys anyway. But this time he was super silent. Beside him was the deputy headteacher, Mrs Garcia. They really were taking this seriously, then.

Mr Matthews signalled for us all to have a seat.

'Now then, everyone,' said Mr Matthews. 'Jackson has something to say to Aisha, don't you, Jackson?'

Jackson ever so slowly raised his head. His eyes were red and puffy and his whole face was blotchy and wet with tears. 'Sorry, Aisha . . .' he whispered. 'It was me. I took your card'

'That's it, Jackson, well done for owning up . . .' said Mrs Garcia.

41

Owning up?! Owning up?! He wouldn't have admitted it if we hadn't found him out in the first place.

That's what I wanted to yell. But I didn't because I was scared of Mr Matthews and also Jackson did look as if the guilt had already Mega-Mashed him to bits anyway.

Aisha looked at me as if to say sorry too. Maybe she shouldn't have jumped to conclusions, but I was totally glad she would be my best friend again, so I smiled back at her.

Jimmy jumped up and punched the air and said, 'I'm freeeeeee!' Then quickly sat back down again with a, 'Sorry, sorry, sorry.' The effort to do self-control could only go so far with Jimmy. I'm surprised he'd lasted that long, to be honest.

'Now, then,' said Mr Matthews laying his hands on the table. 'Here's what we're going to do. I'm going to telephone Jackson's parents and ask them to come in to discuss things further. And Jackson, I can see how sorry you are, but what you did was very wrong, so you will be doing your work outside my office for the rest of the week.'

Now that really *was* a punishment. To sit at the 'Table of Shame' in the corridor outside Mr Matthews's office whilst everyone went by, staring and knowing.

'And we shall have to see about getting that card safely returned to Aisha,' Mr Matthews continued. 'Unfortunately, I will also now have to place a ban on these collector cards coming in to school, as it all seems to have got quite out of hand.'

'What?' cried Jimmy.

I glared at him and he shrank back down in his seat.

'It's for the best, Jimmy, I'm afraid,' explained Mr Matthews. 'Perhaps you can trade them with your friends at one another's houses or in the park at the weekends, that kind of thing.'

After that, all of us, apart from Jackson,

were sent back to class. Once we were out in the corridor, we all heaved a sigh of relief.

'Phew!' said Jimmy. 'That was intense.'

'I'm really sorry, Jimmy, that you got the blame and all that,' said Aisha.

'It's OK, Aish. I forgive ya.'

Jimmy was kind like that.

'And I'm really sorry, Cally, for . . . well . . . you know . . .'

'It's all right, Aisha. I'm just glad we're friends again,' I said.

'Besties for ever?'

'Besties for ever!'

Might I have done the same if I'd been in her place? Possibly. Probably. And anyway, she more than made up for it. When her TTT card was returned to her (and Der-Boy's Cyber Trader page went down – they say Dermot even got a warning from the police), Aisha did the nicest thing ever. She got her mum to put it in a special frame and she gave it to Jimmy!

'Whoa! Really?' said Jimmy, clutching the frame tightly and hopping from one foot to the other.

'It can be both of ours. We can share it. But you can keep it at your house for as long as you like.'

And that's how my twin Jimmy managed to get what he wanted – again.

TRICK-OR-TREAT TWINS

'What's the best day of the year?' Jimmy asked me one morning over breakfast. He's always asking random questions like that.

'That's easy. Our birthday, of course,' I said.

'Not including our birthday, though,' he said.

'All right then, it's obviously Christmas,' I said.

'Noooo. Apart from Christmas as well.'

'What you on about, Jimmy?'

'Say "Halloweeeeeeen"!' he said eagerly.

'Well, yeah, Halloween is cool,' I agreed. And

Halloween was coming up. The supermarket already had a whole aisle dedicated to it – costumes, face paints, decorations, giant tubs of sweets . . .

'I'm gonna be a werewolf,' said Jimmy.

'You're *always* a werewolf,' I said.

'I know. That's why I'm gonna be it again,' he said.

Jimmy suits being a werewolf. He has this wolf hood with crazy sticky-up hair and the costume comes with furry gloves and feet as well. They all still fit. Over the years he just wears bigger black trousers and tops to go with it. He loves getting into that costume. It gives him an excuse to be wild without anyone telling him off, because that's how werewolves are meant to be. So he can go howling through the streets until bedtime if he wants to. Which is, of course, what he always does when it's Halloween.

'What are you going to be this year, Cals?' he asked.

 50

'I think I might be a Day of the Dead senorita,' I said.

'A what?'

'The Day of the Dead. It's a festival they do in Mexico to remember friends and family who have died. They dress up sort of like fancy skeletons, with flowers and stylish clothes. Like, the men have top hats and the girls have veils and frilly Spanish skirts.'

'Trust you to do something clever.'

'Well they've got the outfits in Superco, anyway.'

Yiayia came to the table with a plate of halloumi on toast and sat down to join us for breakfast.

'You'll take us trick-or-treating again won't you, Yiayia?' said Jimmy.

Our street's great for trick-or-treating. Loads of houses put pumpkins in the windows so we can get sweets from them. We go to nearly every house there is. All except for number thirteen. People say the number thirteen is unlucky, don't they? Well, this house looks as if it's had all the bad luck in the world. Number thirteen is creepy. Like it's Halloween there all year round. The garden's overgrown, the gate's all rusty, the paint's peeling off the walls, the windows are rotten, and the old lady who lives inside looks like she might really be a witch. She's as thin as a stick, her hair is long, wispy and grey, and her face is all sunken and caved-in. She hardly ever comes out; she just appears at the window, staring onto the street, watching.

'Is Halloween already?' said Yiayia.

'Well, technically not until next month,' I explained, 'but Jimmy's planning it from now.'

Trick-or-treating is a big deal to Jimmy. Especially as he's not usually allowed that many sweets because they make him too 'lively' – that's the polite word the grown-ups use for 'hyper'. But when it's trick-or-treat time, there's so much candy everywhere, Jimmy manages to get away with having more than usual. I'm in charge of holding our bucket for collecting all the goodies. It's in the shape of a giant pumpkin. We're not meant to eat too much as we're going around the houses. We have to hand our stash over to Mum when we get back home and she shares the treats out bit by bit over time. I think she secretly eats half of them herself.

'So you're coming trick-or-treating with us then, Yiayia?' said Jimmy again.

'Yes, yes, I come,' said Yiayia, squishing Jimmy's cheek.

Yiayia's too cute. She even wears a mask at Halloween to join in with it properly. It's

Jimmy's. One of those *Scream* ones – white, with big hollow black eyes and a long open mouth, like in that famous painting and the emojis. We always tell her she doesn't have to dress up. But she mostly wears black anyway and the mask seems to go with it quite well. Yiayia's pretty small, so she looks like she's just another one of the kids.

★

A few weeks later, when it finally got to the actual day of Halloween, Jimmy was beside himself with excitement. After school we got straight into our costumes, ready for trick-or-treating. Jimmy was being extra annoying, because he couldn't wait to go out.

'Why do we have to wait until dark?' he said, hopping up and down at the window.

'Because that's when spooky stuff goes on, isn't it? When have you ever seen a horror movie that happens in broad daylight?'

'When have *you* ever seen a horror movie ever, anyway? You're such a wimp you can't even watch *Goosebumps* without hiding behind a pillow.'

But before it could turn into a full-blown argument, Yiayia poked her head round the living-room door, wearing her *Scream* mask, and said, 'Boo!' We all cracked up.

'How about we play some Halloween games until it gets dark?' I suggested.

'Yeah. We could do apple bobbing,' said Jimmy.

'No way,' I said, remembering what happened last year when Jimmy dunked my head right into the washing-up bowl and almost drowned me. 'I'm not falling for that one again. And anyway, it would ruin my make up.' I'd done my own Day of the Dead face paint design, and I don't want to sound big-headed or anything, but I think I did a really amazingly artistic job of it.

'You always have to be such a spoilsport, Cally. What else are we supposed to play on Halloween?' said Jimmy.

'You want play scare game? I show you Greek-people scare game,' said Yiayia. And she went over to search through her basket where she keeps her knitting and her prayer beads and all her other bits and bobs.

 56

She pulled out a large, flat, round ornament with a leather string for hanging it up with. It was made of blue glass and had a white circle with a black  dot in the middle of it. 'If we is to play scare game, first we must to have this. This is *to mati*. In English is say *evil eye*. We hang this things on wall for keep away evil spirit. We play game to see if you have curse of evil eye on you. Yes?'

That evil eye thing gave me the shivers. 'I meant like, *fun* Halloween games?' I said.

'Always such a chicken, Cally,' said Jimmy. 'So, tell us, Yiayia, how do you know if you've been got by the curse of the evil eye, then?'

'We put drop of oil in glass of water. If floats, is no curse. But if sinks. Is curse.'

'Cool. Let's do it,' said Jimmy, rushing into the kitchen to get a glass of water and the bottle

of olive oil that we're meant to use on the salad, not for testing for evils.

'Do Cally first,' said Jimmy, plonking the glass of water on the table and handing Yiayia the bottle of oil.

'Why me?' I said.

'Cos you're the oldest, as you're always telling everyone.'

'Only by seventeen minutes and forty-two seconds.'

'Well, you always say that counts. So oldest first.'

'Oh . . . all right then. Let's just get on with it. Anyway, everyone knows that oil always floats cos it's less dense than water.' I'd learned that from my *Super Science Facts* book.

Jimmy acted like he already knew that too.

Anyway, we all went very quiet and serious when Yiayia poured the drop of oil into the glass. And when it stayed floating on the surface, we all said, 'Phew!'

I ran to the sink and emptied the glass and filled it with fresh water again. It was Jimmy's turn now. Yiayia got ready to pour in the oil once more. Jimmy did that thing he does of sticking his tongue out the side of his mouth when he's trying really hard to concentrate.

'If there's a curse for being the most-annoying-brother-in-the-whole-wide-world, then you've already got it anyway,' I said.

'Ha, ha, very funny. *Not*,' said Jimmy.

Yiayia poured the oil. It floated. We all said, 'Phew,' again.

'What would happen if it really did sink though?' asked Jimmy.

'Is you have to get Greek mama to say secret prayer for you. Then when you make like yawn, it's show curse is leave you.'

Me and Jimmy both burst out laughing.

Yiayia looked at us with a straight face. 'Why you laugh? Is true.'

Yiayia has tonnes of old lady tales like that.

'What else do the Greeks believe in, then? Tell us another Halloweeny one,' said Jimmy.

Yiayia looked around the room at all the decorations we'd put up for Halloween for inspiration. She pointed to the paper chain of bats hanging at the window and said, 'You know what is bring good luck? Is bones of bat.'

'Whaaaattt?' said Jimmy.

'Is what Greek people believe,' said Yiayia. 'They like to carry bones in pockets or purses. Even some people do chew on bones of bat. That is bring most good luck of all.'

'Eeeeeeeeewwwwwwww!' I said. 'That's so gross.'

'Are you just winding us up now, Yiayia?' said Jimmy.

'You ask to know Greek people story. I tell you Greek people story,' she said.

'Tell us another one, then,' said Jimmy.

'I don't think I can take any more,' I groaned.

'No to worry, Calista mou. We no need to be scared of Devil . . .'

'Who said anything about the Devil?' I said.

'Because all we have to do is make like spit three times. Like this, *ftou . . . ftou . . . ftou . . .*'

Yiayia demonstrated making the spitting sound. I know it sounds crazy, but I've seen old Greek people do it before. Not actual spit, but pretending to. Even in church. Especially in church, actually. Like when there's a christening.

'Is three times spit,' explained Yiayia. '*Ftou*. One for Father. *Ftou*. One for Son. *Ftou*. And one for Holy Ghost. Is to keep Devil away.'

'And I thought all we needed was a pumpkin at Halloween to scare away evil spirits,' I said.

 61

Jimmy thought it was hilarious. 'No harm in a few extra *ftou-ftou-ftous* just to make sure, hey?' And he and Yiayia started going round the room, pretend-spitting on the Devil and any evil spirits that might be lurking under the sofa or behind the curtains.

All that mucking around with weird Greek superstitions did make the time fly though, and soon it was dark enough to go out trick-or-treating. I grabbed the pumpkin bucket for collecting our goodies and we set off to terrorise the neighbourhood. It had been raining all day but luckily it had stopped by the evening. The roads and pavements glistened in the moonlight, which I thought added to the Halloweeny feeling. Yiayia wasn't so keen on all the puddles though, and kept telling Jimmy to be more careful or his furry werewolf feet would get soaked. Jimmy? Careful? As if.

There were loads of other kids out in the streets too. Everyone was squealing and shrieking and laughing and rushing about, on a mission to stock up on sweets before the houses ran out. We bumped into quite a few people from our class along the way. Not my best friend Aisha, though, which was a shame. Her mum and dad are not into Halloween.

63

Mitch Moran bombed past us, with his Dracula cloak flapping behind him, almost knocking Yiayia off her feet. Mitch Moran doesn't exactly have the best manners.

We saw Candice Solomon too. She was dressed as a cat and was out with her brother who was being a zombie.

'Wow, cool costume, Cally. What have you come as?' Candice asked. She was admiring my awesome make-up, I could tell.

'I'm a Day of the Dead senorita,' I said.

I was about to explain all about the festival in Mexico but her brother was already off to the next house with Candice chasing after him, yelling, 'Hey, wait for me!'

We went from house to house looking for the ones with pumpkins on their windowsills or doorsteps. Our neighbours were really generous and had plenty of treats to share with us. Jimmy managed to scoff more than he was meant to as we went around, of course, and he was becoming more and more wild. Jumping and dancing about, howling his head off.

Far too many artificial additives, Mum would have said. The people at number fifteen would have agreed as they had very proudly made organic, vegan monster cupcakes to share out that evening. They had actual pumpkin in them too. They looked really good but they were a bit disgusting. Yuck.

Next door to them was number thirteen with its rusty gate, overgrown garden and tumbledown house. It looked extra gloomy in the dark, with rainwater dripping from its broken gutters. I went to walk straight past, but from a downstairs window came an unexpected glimmer of light.

'Look!' cried Jimmy. 'The witch at number thirteen has put a pumpkin in her window!'

'Who is witch?' asked Yiayia.

'The old lady in number thirteen,' said Jimmy. 'Everyone says she is.'

'Is not kind to call people witch, Jimmy. Is just old lady, like your Yiayia,' she said.

Now that Yiayia put it like that, I did start to feel a little bit guilty.

'But . . . everyone says . . .' said Jimmy weakly.

Why had the old lady put a pumpkin in her window? In all the times we've been trick-or-treating, she'd never done that before.

'So, you go knock on door? Is trick or treat,' said Yiayia.

'No way,' said Jimmy. And he ran howling down the street, looking for the next house that had a pumpkin. A more normal one.

It was getting late now and after we'd visited the last of the houses down our road, we turned back to go home.

'Give us a sweet,' said Jimmy, trying to grab the pumpkin bucket from me.

'No more,' I said, swiping it out of his way. 'You've had a million times more than you're allowed already.'

Jimmy started running around me in circles, trying to get at the bucket.

'Tell him, Yiayia!' I held the bucket high over my head.

Jimmy jumped up at it, looking more like a crazy puppy than a werewolf. He jumped and jumped. Every time he made a grab for it, I backed away. But he still wouldn't give up.

'Stop it, Jimmy!' I said.

But he didn't stop. He kept jumping up and jumping up and then he did the dumbest thing ever. He punched the bucket out of my hands.

'Stop it, Jimmy!'

And all the sweets, the whole lot, went flying through the air. And guess where they landed? Right smack bang in the middle of a giant puddle by the side of the road. And next to a drain as well.

'Look what you've done!' I yelled.

'I only wanted another sweet,' said Jimmy, sheepishly.

'Well now no one's getting any, are they? Why do you always have to ruin everything?' I said, giving him a big, hard shove.

Yiayia, stepped in between us and said, 'All right, all right, is enough now.'

'But Yiayia, there's nothing left,' I said, picking up the now completely empty pumpkin bucket from the pavement.

'Maybe we can knock on a few more doors?' said Jimmy.

'We've already done all the houses. We can't go asking the neighbours for more. We'll look greedy. And anyway, everyone's probably run out of stuff by now,' I said.

'Is one house we not go to yet,' said Yiayia. 'Number thirteen must to maybe have some sweet?'

Me and Jimmy looked at each other.

'Dare you,' I said.

'Dare you, too,' said Jimmy.

'All right, let's both do it together,' I said.

Slowly, in silence, we stepped back along the pavement towards house number thirteen.

Yiayia stopped at the gate.

'Come with us, Yiayia,' said Jimmy.

'No. Is for children, trick-or-treat.' Yiayia

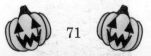

was right. That's what the grown-ups did. They always waited on the street while the kids knocked on the doors. But this time I wouldn't have minded her coming with us.

I pushed open the rusty gate. It creaked on its hinges, like they do in spooky stories. We made our way up the stony path. The weeds either side were taller than us and they brushed against our arms and legs, giving us the shivers. When we got to the door, my hand trembled as I went to press the bell. We stood and waited. Part of me still thought about turning back. But it was too late now. Then came the sound of footsteps shuffling towards us from behind the door. Then the rattling of the chain being undone from the inside. Eventually the door opened, ever so slowly. I forgot to breathe for a few seconds. And there she was. The old lady. Thin as a stick with her wispy hair and big staring eyes.

But do you know what? The moment she

saw us standing there on her doorstep, she gave us a smile. Her teeth were all crooked and her face was all wrinkly, but she actually looked pleased to see us.

We just stood there in stunned silence.

'Aren't you meant to say "Trick or treat"?'
the old lady said.

'Oh, yeah, trick or treat,' said Jimmy.

I held the pumpkin bucket out towards her.

'Trick or treat?'

'Oooh, that looks a bit empty, doesn't it, dear?' she said.

'We dropped it and lost all our sweets,' said Jimmy.

'*We?*' I said, giving him an angry glare.

'It was an accident,' said Jimmy.

'He's always saying that,' I said to the old lady. 'He has a lot of *accidents*!'

'Ah well, not to worry. Let's see what I've got for you. There's plenty here,' she said, reaching for a giant tub of TerrorMix that she had on a table by the door. 'You're the first ones, you know. I'm not sure why. I put a pumpkin in my window this year because no one ever knocks on my door. Someone told me that's what people are meant to do. Is that right? Perhaps I didn't put it in the right place? Maybe it can't be easily seen from outside, my garden's such a mess. Anyway, I'm ever so pleased you came. Here, take as many as you like.'

Jimmy's eyes lit up and he went to grab a big handful.

'Not too many, Jimmy,' I said. 'He's not allowed lots of sugar, you see. It makes him, well, it disagrees with him,' I explained.

'Oh, well, then. Let's see what else we might be able to rustle up for you, shall we?'

'Oh, no, really, that's very kind, but you don't have to . . .'

But the old lady was already shuffling off back inside to see what else she could find. Me and Jimmy looked at each other again.

She was actually really nice, wasn't she? I wondered if Jimmy was feeling as ashamed as I was.

When she came back to the door, she was carrying a little plastic ghost. It had an LED light inside which made it glow from red, to pink, to purple, to green, to blue.

'There now,' she said, 'will this do?'

'Wow, that's so cool. Thank you Mrs . . . Mrs . . . ?'

'Mrs Draper,' she said. And then she must have noticed Yiayia waiting for us back at the gate because she said, 'Doesn't your little brother want to come and get a treat too?'

'Oh no, that's our Yiayia,' laughed Jimmy.

'Our granny,' I explained.

'We call her Yiayia, because she's Greek from Cyprus, except she lives with us now. We're at number ninety-seven.'

'Oh, I see. Go and get her, then. Don't leave her standing up there,' said Mrs Draper.

I went back to the gate and brought Yiayia over to say hello. Yiayia took off her *Scream* mask and shook Mrs Draper's hand.

'How very lovely to meet you,' said Mrs Draper. 'Thank you for coming by with your delightful grandchildren. You're so lucky to have family, it's just me these days.'

Jimmy? Delightful? Mrs Draper must have been *really* lonely.

Even with my facepaint on, I obviously looked a bit sad for Mrs Draper, because she said, 'Oh you mustn't worry about me now, luvvie. There's always the community centre for a bit of company. They do a smashing knitting and natter group, as it happens. I really ought to try to go more often.'

 78

'Oh, you should see our Yiayia. She's always knitting. You could go to that, Yiayia,' I said.

'Knitty natter?' said Yiayia.

'Oh it's just an excuse to get out and have a cup of tea and a chat really. It's every Tuesday at eleven,' explained Mrs Draper.

'Oh yes. Is sound good. We maybe go together next time?' said Yiayia.

'I'd like that very much,' said Mrs Draper. 'Bye for now, then. And Happy Halloween!' she said, as we went off back down her overgrown garden and out through the creaky, rusty gate.

When we got home, Mum looked at our measly collection of sweets. 'You haven't eaten everything already, have you?'

'Oh, no, we lost them all,' said Jimmy. He held up his glow-in-the-dark ghost. 'But we got this.'

'Is true,' said Yiayia.

'And Yiayia got a new friend,' I said.

'Is also true,' said Yiayia.

'Mrs Draper,' I added.

'And she's not even really like a witch at all,' said Jimmy. 'But actually, you can get good witches too, can't you? Maybe Mrs Draper's one of them . . .'

'Jimmy! Stop calling her a witch now. She's just Mrs Draper from number thirteen and that's it,' I said.

But Jimmy carried on. '. . . there's a good witch in *The Wizard of Oz*, isn't there? And what about the one in *Meg and Mog*. She's a nice witch, isn't she . . . ?'

'Let's just keep these thoughts about who might or might not be a witch to ourselves from now on, good or otherwise,' said Mum,

shaking her head. 'You all seem to have had a very eventful Halloween. We'll leave it at that, shall we?'

Mum was right. At the end of it all, as I took off my facepaint in the bathroom, I couldn't help thinking about bat bones and evil eyes, pumpkins in lonely windows and the number thirteen – which they say is unlucky for some, but not, as it turned out, for me and my twin Jimmy.

TRACKTASTIC
TWINS

If there's one thing my twin Jimmy is better at than me, it's sport. I'm pretty much better than Jimmy at everything else. I know that sounds big-headed, but it's true. Especially when it comes to learning and all that. I'm on the top table. Jimmy has to have Miss Loretta to stop him mucking about all the time, or 'to help him focus' as the grown-ups like to call it. I know it's not his fault, really. He has ADHD and that can be awful for him. It's like his head is racing away, all over the place, at a million miles a minute, and he can't sit still, which makes it very hard for him to concentrate. So when it comes to reading, writing and maths, it's really tiring for him to try and keep up with everything. And you should see it whenever there's a test or the school reports come out. It's a nightmare. Most people are kind to Jimmy about it, but he knows he's the worst out of everybody in the whole class. And it doesn't help when some kids like Mitch Moran laugh at him and call him 'Dimmy'. The grown-ups are all very careful with Jimmy, giving him a zillion house points if he manages to get even a few things right. And deep down I know that's nice, but it doesn't feel all that fair when I get the top scores and Mum and Yiayia never make a big deal of it, or even remember to congratulate me, in case Jimmy gets upset.

But Jimmy's definitely the best at sport out of the two of us, 100 per cent. Especially when it comes to running. That's when he gets to really put his hyperness to use. I'm not really allowed to use the word 'hyper'. The grown-ups say there are kinder words for that too. We're supposed to say 'lively'. Anyway, his extra energy gives him a proper head start when it comes to being fast. And that's why he's better than me. And he's better than everyone, really. All except for Mitch Moran, who's just that bit faster than Jimmy whenever we do races. Which is a shame, because it would be nice to see Jimmy come top in something, just once. He might be annoying, but he's still my brother.

It was nearly the end of the summer term, which meant Sports Day was coming. Jimmy especially likes that time of year at school because there are loads of other activities going on which break up all the usual boring lessons. We'd just had a trip to Hampton Court and there was Art Week soon, where we'd get to do loads of fun crafty stuff outside, and the Year Sixes were doing a Leavers' Show that the Year Fives got to help with. Plus there was the

Summer Fair to get things ready for as well. It's good, the summer term. And the highlight for Jimmy would of course be Sports Day.

And then, in assembly, our headteacher Mr Matthews made an announcement that meant Sports Day was going to be extra special this year.

'Now, children, I have some very exciting news for us all,' he began.

There were hushed murmurs, but not too many because Mr Matthews is one of those serious headteachers who all the children sit quietly for, especially in assembly.

'Do you remember earlier in the year how we all had to collect tokens from the Wheatios cereal boxes?' he asked us.

Do I remember? How could I forget? It was Jimmy's major obsession for weeks. He doesn't even like Wheatios, and neither do I. Wheatios are like cardboard. You're supposed to make them taste nicer by putting sweet things on, like maple syrup, but Jimmy's not allowed much sugar, so I have to sacrifice it too, because we're twins and it wouldn't be fair. Yiayia sometimes lets me have a bit of her special Greek honey to put on them that her brother, Bapou Nikos sends over from Cyprus, but we'd run out.

So basically, we had to eat disgusting Wheatios for two whole months because Jimmy wanted to be the one to collect the most tokens

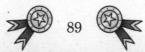

for school. There was a prize for the person who did, but Jimmy couldn't even win that. Candice Solomon's mum works at the recycling factory and she'd gone through all the Wheatios boxes, cutting out the spare tokens, so Candice totally smashed it. The point of collecting the tokens was that schools could exchange them for sports equipment. But also, the school with the most, would win a real, live Olympic athlete to come to their Sports Day.

'And it is largely because of Candice Solomon's enterprise,' continued Mr Matthews, 'that I am extremely pleased to announce that our school has won!'

Everybody whooped and cheered. Mr Matthews stood smartly at the front of the hall watching us and waiting until we quietened down again. He then put a picture up on the big screen of a skinny, yet totally muscly athlete in a Great Britain kit, tearing through the ribbon of a finish line with his arms open.

He had a badge on his vest that said his name: Kerubo. He looked very cool but I don't think any of us knew who he was because there weren't any more 'Oohs' and 'Aahs' coming from the children. I think Mr Matthews expected we might not have heard of him, because he had lots more photos and a video clip to show us as he went on to explain who our special guest athlete was.

'This is Yusuf Kerubo, or Yu Kerubo as he was known, back in the nineteen-nineties when he was a big star for the GB athletic team. He's won golds in both the hundred metre and two hundred metre sprints for several of the major tournaments, including the Olympics. His parents are from Kenya, but he grew up nearby in Brentford.'

That's a bit like our mum. Mum's parents are Greek from Cyprus, but she was born in Shepherd's Bush. Mum's dad, or Bapou Vasilis as we called him, died when me and Jimmy were little and we can't really remember him, but I think living with us stops Yiayia missing Bapou quite so much.

It soon became clear that even if the kids didn't know who Yu Kerubo was, the mums and dads definitely did.

'Oh wow! Really?' gasped Mum, when we told her. 'Yu Kerubo is going to be at your Sports Day? He was a big star once, you know.'

Even Yiayia had heard of him. She turned the house upside down searching for her autograph book. 'Is famous people is Yo Korob. Must to be get him to sign.'

'Do you think he'll watch all the races, Mum?' asked Jimmy. 'Do you think he'll notice how fast I am?'

'That would be good, wouldn't it, Jimmy? Let's hope so,' said Mum, ruffling his hair.

'I'm going to do extra training on the rec after school,' said Jimmy, flexing his muscles. The rec's what we call this bit of green in front of our house. It's where people mostly go to exercise their dogs, but Jimmy likes to go out there and do laps round it too.

Sometimes he pretends to be a train. He can do impressions of all the different tube rides on the London Underground. The Victoria line is his favourite sound at the moment. Mum and Yiayia let him run about on the rec on his own as we can easily see him from the window. They say it's good for him to use up all that extra energy he has. But I think it's really because they need to have a bit of a break from Jimmy too. Even if he is their favourite.

Jimmy had been chosen for the sprint. The most important race. I didn't think Yu Kerubo would be quite so impressed with mine. I'd been put in one of the novelty races for the non-sporty kids. And not even one of the good ones, like the three-legged race or the sack race. They don't do the egg-and-spoon any more because there were too many ways of cheating, like putting your thumb over the egg to keep it on the spoon – once a kid even got caught using Blu Tack to stick his down.

No, my race was the wheelbarrow. It might actually have been fun if an actual proper wheelbarrow was involved, and you could ride down the tracks in it for real. But no. The *people* have to be the wheelbarrows. You do it with a partner. You put your hands on the ground, as if you're about to do a handstand, and then you kick your feet up and the other person holds onto your legs. Then you walk on your hands all the way to the finish line. It totally kills your arms. At least my partner was my best friend Aisha. That was the only thing that made it just about bearable. We'd practised together a bit at lunchtimes, but then Mitch Moran ran past and said he could see my knickers, so we stopped after that.

But Jimmy practised all the time. He so wanted to win that sprint. Every day, as soon as we got home from school, he'd get changed into his shorts and T-shirt, put his trainers on and head out for the rec.

Mum's friend Grant was round one afternoon. And of course he had to try and get involved. He's this fix-it man who comes over to help with stuff like painting and putting up shelves, even when there isn't any painting to be done or shelves to be put up. Me and Jimmy think he fancies Mum. We find him really cringe. Anyway, know-it-all that he is, Grant started bragging about how he was some sort of expert in sports too.

'Did you know, Jimmy,' he said, 'that I used to be quite the athlete, back in the day?'

'Ooh, that's impressive isn't it, Jimmy?' said Mum.

Jimmy was more interested in putting his trainers on so he could get out to the rec. He was concentrating on tying his laces, doing that thing he does of sticking his tongue out the side of his mouth when he's trying really hard at something. Laces are a big deal to Jimmy – he's only just learned how to do them.

So Grant carried on showing off to Mum about it instead. Puffing up his chest and flexing his muscles. 'Yes, Stella,' he said to Mum. 'Hundred metre sprint, two hundred metres, the four hundred, long distance, you name it. Even competed in the nationals, you know?'

Mum practically swooned. Yiayia gave a really big yawn and shuffled off, saying she was tired. That made me laugh. She wasn't tired at all. She found Grant as irritating as we did.

'Maybe Grant could help you with your training, Jimmy?' said Mum. 'Give you a few tips?'

Grant was already practically limbering up by the front door, doing this weird high-knees action and stretching his arms out to the side, nearly knocking the plants off the windowsill.

'Nah. It's OK,' said Jimmy. 'Dad's gonna help me when we go to his at the weekend.'

And Grant stopped doing his dumb fancy moves, picked up his toolbag and went off to the kitchen to find something else to fix.

Dad did help Jimmy over the weekend when we went to stay with him. I didn't mind too much as I knew how important it was for Jimmy, but it was sort of annoying as well because we don't get to see Dad that much and literally the whole weekend was spent on Clapham Common, with Jimmy getting all the attention.

They practised the right starting position for ages, and then I had to watch Jimmy do lap after lap round the pond with Dad timing him on a stopwatch he'd bought specially. To be fair to Dad, he did say he would help me practise for my race too – but being a wheelbarrow was humiliating enough as it was for Sports Day. I didn't feel like making a fool of myself in front of the whole of Clapham on a Saturday afternoon as well.

★

The big day arrived. It was a Friday afternoon and the hottest day of the year, according to all the teachers who wouldn't stop going on about it the whole time. Sun hats, sun cream, plenty of water, over and over again. The staff were taking it extra seriously this year because of our special guest. They'd made us practise our races all week in PE, so my arms were aching like mad from being the rubbish wheelbarrow.

 100

We'd been taught our lining up orders so exactly, it was like we were in the army, not at school. It was all worth it though, because as we marched out onto the field, all kitted out in our red, blue, green and yellow house colours to take our places by the side of the track, it felt so exciting. Me and Jimmy are both in Red House. I think it's the teachers' way of trying to keep things fair for us. Just because we're twins, it doesn't mean we *have* to be the same. In so many ways, we're totally different.

We both know that. Even if we are made to wear the same colour T-shirt on Sports Day. Just as well we're in Red House, though. It's Jimmy's favourite colour. So it totally matters to him.

The smell of freshly cut grass wafted into the air and everyone was wowed by the newly painted track lines. They looked very professional. The crowd was super massive – practically the whole of West London had turned up – not a single mum, dad, auntie, uncle, grandma or grandad wanted to miss *this* year's special Sports Day. Even Jackson Boyle's mum was there.

Mr Matthews stood at the front under a string of bunting, with a big funnel-shaped megaphone in his hand. It made his voice sound like a robot and it was such an ancient piece of equipment, no one could properly hear him anyway. But he used it every year.

Even after the invention of proper speakers and microphones. He was very proud of it. No one was ever allowed to touch it except him. Placing it in front of his face like an oversized trumpet, he made the announcement we had all been waiting for: 'Ladies and gentlemen, girls and boys, it is a great honour to introduce our very special guest, who will be opening our Sports Day event. Please give a warm welcome to Yu Kerubo!' Or that's what I think he said.

And then out he sprang. The great superstar himself. He was about a hundred years old, with grey hair, but he was as lively and as bouncy as the young athlete we'd seen in the videos. I wondered if Jimmy would still be like that when he was ancient too. Most probably.

The crowd cheered so loudly, it was as if we were actually at the Olympics. Us children were being pretty well-behaved because the teachers had made it clear that we had to stay in our places at all times. We would get a chance to line up for autographs, class by class, later in the day.

But you should have seen the parents! Jackson's mum was up out of her seat and shouting from across the track, 'Jackson, Jackson, go get him to sign your shirt!' Jackson went bright red and tried to hide inside his vest. She carried on waving her arms at Jackson and pointing like crazy towards where Yu Kerubo was. Everyone in our class started giggling.

Mr Matthews had all sorts of professional Sports Day gadgets saved up for this special

occasion, including a real-life starter pistol. Normally no one else was allowed to touch that either. Except this time, of course, Yu Kerubo was the one in charge of starting the races. The first of the Year Three groups was in place at the top of the track and the races were about to begin. A row of small children stood there, in serious concentration, each with a beanbag balanced on their head, as Yu Kerubo raised the pistol in the air and said, 'On your marks, get set, go!'

He fired the gun and they were off.

Jimmy was itching for it to be his turn. He so wanted to impress Yu Kerubo. He gazed at the track and said, 'I really hope I win.'

'I hope you win too, Jimmy,' I said.

Mitch Moran butted in. 'Don't get your hopes up, Dimmy. Even if you have been in training. Yeah, I saw you running round the rec, making choo-choo train noises like an idiot.'

Jimmy hugged himself and looked down into his lap.

'Who asked you, Mitch?' I said.

Mitch just shrugged and pulled a face.

It was still ages till the Year Five races anyway. So we'd just have to wait and see.

Sports Day can be fun, and yes it was extra special because we had Yu Kerubo this year, but there is also a *lot* of waiting around and doing nothing too. You only get to be in one race, maybe two if you're lucky, and the whole rest of the time is just waiting about for it to be your turn and being told a million times by the teacher to stay sitting down and that you're not allowed to go and see your parents until the end – which was especially frustrating for me and Jimmy, cos we could see Dad right there across the field and we don't see him as much as some kids see their dads, so all we really wanted to do was go and sit with him. I'm sure Dad felt the same. In fact, I bet all the parents did. They only really come to watch their own kids, don't they? Except for the super-competitive ones who seem to live for the parents' race at the end.

Mum and Yiayia were there as well. They sat next to Dad because Mum says they can be civilised like that. Yiayia had brought her little folding chair and her knitting with her – she knew how much waiting around there was too. She was always prepared for these things. She had her cool bag at her feet as well, packed with a tonne of Greek pastries and biscuits, spanakopita, tiropita, koulourakia . . . 'Everybody needs eat,' she'd insisted.

Jackson Boyle was probably one of the few children who would rather his mum hadn't been

there, though. Maybe she wanted to make more of an effort to come along to things since the TTT card disaster, but I bet Jackson would have preferred that she'd stayed away like before, cos she was being really embarrassing. She kept going up to Yu Kerubo in between races with her smartphone, trying to get a selfie with him. I couldn't hear what Mr Matthews said to her, but by the look on his face and the way he pointed back to the parents' seating area the third time she tried, he really wasn't pleased. Worse still, on her way back to her place, she bumped into the table which had Mr Matthews's precious megaphone on, sending it crashing to the ground. Mr Matthews looked like he might explode. Jackson was almost dying by this point. The rest of us were laughing our heads off.

Finally, the time came for me and Aisha to take our places at the track. Not that I was in any hurry to make a fool of myself in front of the whole school, not to mention a real Olympian

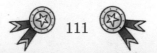

superstar. But at least it meant I could get up off the mat and it did mean I got to see Yu Kerubo properly. He wished us all luck and gave us a giant smile that took up almost the whole of his face. I liked him. I wanted to say sorry in advance for the performance I was about to give. I knew it wouldn't be my finest moment.

'On your marks . . .'

I placed my palms on the ground and kicked my feet up.

'Get set . . .'

Aisha took firm hold of my legs.

'Go!'

Yu Kerubo fired the starter pistol and off we went. Right from the start, we found ourselves trailing behind the others.

'Come on, Calista mou!'

Yiayia was cheering from the sidelines and waving a Cyprus flag.

It didn't help. The gap between us and the rest of the Year Five wheelbarrows was just getting bigger and bigger with every painful, embarrassing second. My arms got weaker and weaker until they felt like jelly. I collapsed to the ground, my nose in the grass.

'Come on, Cally!' yelled Aisha.

Almost everyone else had finished the race and we hadn't even made it halfway down the track. And there I was, looking like the world's worst smashed-up wheelbarrow ever.

'I can't,' I cried.

And then, Aisha did the wackiest thing. She scooped her arms around the tops of my legs and picked me right up. Little, skinny Aisha. No one could believe

it. What must it have looked like? Me, upside down, being carried along the field by my best friend. I started paddling my arms really fast in the air to make it seem as if I was at least doing some kind of wheelbarrowing.

It must have looked hilarious because the whole crowd was laughing – but not in a horrible way. And everyone really cheered and clapped for us when we crossed the finish line.

Mrs Wright was there at the end giving out stickers. Obviously the first, second and third place ones were long gone, but she had tears in her eyes as she gave me and Aisha each a yellow smiley face for effort.

Next up was the Year Five sprint race. Jimmy's big moment. I rushed back to my mat with the rest of the class, ready to cheer him on. I so badly wanted him to win, just this once. But Mitch Moran was there. And Mitch Moran was good. Mitch Moran always won.

A hush fell across the whole field as the Year Five sprinters got into position. I swear I saw Mitch looking at Jimmy. Probably saying something nasty to him again. Trying to put him off. If Mitch was going to win, he could at least be a good sport about it.

'On your marks . . .'

I crossed my fingers for Jimmy.

'Get set . . .'

Come on, Jimmy, I prayed.

 115

'Go . . .'

And they were off. There were eight children in the race, but basically it was just Jimmy and Mitch. They were metres ahead of everyone else.

They were neck and neck. It was going to be close.

Then, as if he had some sort of super-sonic-turbo-booster inside him, Jimmy broke ahead.

'Come on, Jimmy!'

Jimmy was winning. All that practice was paying off. There was at least a metre between him and Mitch now and the gap was getting ever so slightly bigger and bigger with every stride.

The cheers from the crowds were getting louder and louder. Yiayia was practically waving her flag off its stick, crying, 'Haddeh, Jimmy mou, haddeh!' Jimmy was going to win. Jimmy really was going to win.

And then, the absolute worst thing ever happened. I watched it all take place as if in slow motion, as Jimmy, just metres before the finish line, tripped, flew tragically through the air, and came crashing devastatingly to the ground. Mitch Moran zipped past him and crossed the finish line, first, as always. The only one cheering for Mitch was his mum.

Everyone else was gasping and shaking their heads and saying things like, 'Poor Jimmy,' and, 'So unfair,' and, 'Is he all right?'

Of course Jimmy wasn't all right. He was able to pick himself up, so he hadn't sprained his ankle or cut himself or anything like that. But he was deeply, deeply hurt inside. This was the worst kind of pain for Jimmy. Being his twin, I really felt it. They say twins do that sometimes – like they have something called 'telepathy', or is it 'empathy'? Or maybe both. Whatever. All I knew was that Jimmy was completely gutted. Even though it was against the rules to get up off the mats, I automatically found myself running onto the track to help him. But he'd curled himself up so tightly into a ball I couldn't get through to him. Miss Loretta, our teaching assistant, who is mainly Jimmy's helper, came over too.

'It's OK, Cally. I'll look after Jimmy. You go back to sit with your class now,' she said.

Miss Loretta prised Jimmy up off the track. Tears were rolling down his cheeks – he couldn't even speak, he was that upset. People patted him on the back as he went by, but he shrugged everyone off and his face started to turn to thunder. Miss Loretta knows that look only too well and so she steered him away from the crowds and took him inside for some quiet time.

Jimmy missed the rest of the races. There were only the Year Six ones left and the parents' race to go anyway. I was glad about that as we really had been sitting around for way too long; even the teachers had given up on getting us to be all organised in tidy rows.

Finally, it was time for the parents' race. Luckily Mum and Dad don't go in for that sort of thing. Dad doesn't like too much attention and Mum says she's always very tired, so there was no way they would be running. I used to really want them to when I was little, but it would be way too cringe now that I'm in Year Five.

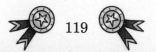

One year, Yiayia nearly offered after Jimmy went on and on at Mum and Dad to join in. A grannies and grandads race – now that *would* be interesting. I could just imagine Yiayia jogging down the track, with her handbag hooked over her arm and her knitting trailing behind her, waving at everyone as she went by. But there's nothing funny about the parents' race. The ones who enter take it super seriously.

There they all were now, trying to get to the best lane and doing all these fancy warm-up stretches. One of the dads even had proper running shorts and a vest like Yu Kerubo wore in the video clips. He'd had them on underneath his tracksuit for the whole afternoon, waiting for this big moment. He had actual running spikes too. Candice Solomon's mum was taking part as well. I wondered if she'd win the parents' race for Candice as well as the Wheetios tokens competition. It looked for a minute like Jackson's mum was getting up to join in too.

I could see Jackson shrinking into the ground as if willing it to swallow him up. Luckily for him, his mum was only shoving her way to  the front to get a better view.

The parents all got into position. Half of them were doing that professional sprint start on the ground, where you have to get on all fours. I reckon they were showing off for Yu Kerubo. Yu Kerubo raised the starter pistol in the air, and for the last time that day said, 'On your marks . . . get set . . . go!'

And off the parents went. I found myself cheering for Candice's mum, cos Candice is my friend. She was doing quite well. Beating the dad in the running spikes at least, and she only had normal trainers on. And then, suddenly the crowd started cheering extra loudly.

That's when I noticed Yu Kerubo had started running down the track with them. He caught the mums and dads up, even though they'd all had quite a head start, and sprinted past them to cross the finish line, ending the race with a cartwheel and a backflip. We all whooped and cheered and clapped. Someone's mum out of the Year Threes crossed the finish line next, but Yu Kerubo was the real superstar.

How great to see him in action. It's a shame Jimmy was still inside and missed it.

After the races were over, Mr Matthews picked up his muffled megaphone to make an announcement. 'And that concludes this afternoon's races. Thank you everyone for participating with such . . . err . . . verve and enthusiasm. We will now have a bit of a break so that we can add up all the team points to see which house has won this year's Sports Day trophy. Parents may join their children and there are refreshments for those who'd like to purchase them, kindly organised by the PSA, at the far end of the field by the huts. Yu Kerubo will also be providing autographs and the children are invited to line up with their families, class by class, starting with Year Three. Thank you.' Well, that's what I think he said!

At last, I was allowed to go and see Dad, Mum and Yiayia. I rushed over and gave Dad the biggest hug.

'Did you see my wheelbarrow, Dad? It was crazy, wasn't it? Did you see when Aisha picked me up?'

'Hilarious,' he laughed.

'Such a shame about poor Jimmy, though,' said Mum.

'I know, he so nearly won,' I agreed.

'But where is to be Jimmy?' said Yiayia.

'He's still inside with Miss Loretta, I think,' I said.

'I'll go and look for him,' said Mum. 'You go with Yiayia and get your autographs done.'

'Shall I come with you to see Jimmy?' Dad asked Mum.

'Noooo, Dad. Come with us,' I said, tugging at his arm. I know Jimmy was having a really bad day, but he didn't have to have both our parents all to himself. It was my Sports Day too.

Dad ruffled my hair. 'OK then, Cals. Let's go meet the famous Yu Kerubo, then.'

124

It was a long queue for Yu Kerubo. Jackson's mum was trying to get in at the front with Jackson, even though it was the Year Fours' turn at the time. I saw Yu Kerubo politely asking her to wait in line with the others, but she just stayed where she was anyway.

While me and Dad queued up with Yiayia, she showed us her autograph book. She'd found it in the end, in the biscuit tin of all places. I didn't recognise any of the signatures, but she very proudly told us all about the people behind them. 'This one here, is Hambis Haralambides. Owner of halloumi factory. Serve halloumi to all supermarkets, not just Cyprus, but London too.' There were several Greek singers and bouzouki band players, the President of Cyprus from 1982 and even the Archbishop. ' . . . He visit Saint Nicholas Church. Is very important, is Archbishop. Archbishop is like king, you know?'

At last it was our turn to meet Yu Kerubo.

He was sitting at the table where Mr Matthews kept his megaphone and the trophy. He looked up and smiled, even though he'd been signing autographs for ages.

'And your name is . . . ?'

'I'm Cally, short for Calista . . .'

'That's a Greek name, isn't it?' he said, noticing Yiayia.

Yiayia looked very pleased. 'Greek from Cyprus,' she nodded.

I had a photo of Yu Kerubo that I'd printed from the internet and he started signing it for me. 'Can you write it to Jimmy as well? He's my twin brother. He's the boy who tripped up in his race when he nearly won. He got upset, so he's with our mum at the moment.'

'That's nice of you to think about your brother,' said Yu Kerubo.

'Well, he's my twin. I'm supposed to. And it was sad that he fell over and Mitch won instead. Jimmy never wins anything, and he'd been training really hard. It's not fair really.'

'Yes, that is a shame,' he agreed. 'I saw your brother run. He was very good. Great technique.' Then he grinned. 'And I remember your race too. An interesting version of the wheelbarrow.'

That's when I went bright red and said, 'Thanks, you can sign my yiayia's one now.'

After a good break and once all the autographs had been signed, Mr Matthews

announced that it was time for the awards ceremony. We were allowed to sit on the field with our parents now that all the races were over. I sat next to Dad, and Jimmy was cuddled up between Mum and Yiayia. His face was still a bit red and blotchy from all the crying he'd been doing, and he looked tired out, like he usually does after a big meltdown.

Even though there were hundreds of us, Mr Matthews managed to command hush over the field with his megaphone. But no one could hear him properly cos that instrument was so muffly and crackly and useless. It seemed to be getting worse as the day went on. And then it suddenly died completely. I think the batteries might have run out or something. Which was a good thing really, because Mrs Garcia, our deputy headteacher, blew a whistle to get everyone's attention instead, which worked much better.

Mr Matthews used his big loud voice, which

was absolutely fine anyway now that we were all sitting closely together, to make the end of the day speeches. 'Ladies and gentlemen, girls and boys, it is now time to announce this year's winners of the house trophy. But before I do so, may I commend everyone who took part so sportingly. Remember that it is the taking part and not the winning that matters above all . . .'

Try telling that to Mitch Moran or the dad with the running spikes.

'I would also of course like to thank all the members of staff for preparing the children and coordinating this event so excellently.'

There was a round of applause for our teachers and our TAs and the premises manager and Mrs Johnston, who does first aid and lost property.

'We must also say a big thank you to the PSA and all the parents who have come to support us today.'

Another round of applause.

'But above all, the biggest thank you must go to our special guest, who it has been an absolute privilege to have with us today, our very own local hero, Yu Kerubo!'

The field erupted into whoops and cheers. Everyone loved Yu Kerubo. Yu Kerubo was great.

'And now, without further ado . . .' Mr Matthews always says fancy things when he's making big announcements like *without*

further ado. ' . . . It is time to declare this year's winning house of the Sports Day trophy.'

Mrs Garcia was in charge of adding up the points, and she handed Mr Matthews a clipboard with the final scores.

'And the winners are . . . Blue House.'

A quarter of the people on the field cheered. Everyone else did polite clapping.

Jimmy folded his arms and said, 'Looks like we're winning nothing today, then.'

And then, just as Mr Matthews looked as if he was about to do his wrapping-things-up speech about how we all needed to return to our teachers and file sensibly back to our classrooms to collect our bags and stuff and then meet our parents safely in the front playground, Yu Kerubo stepped forward as if he wanted to say something too.

'I would like to just add a few words if I may,' he said. 'First of all, I must extend my thanks to Mr Matthews and all the staff, parents and children for giving me such a great day here with you all.' There was another round of applause. 'And now, I too have an award that I would like to present.'

Mr Matthews and Mrs Garcia looked at each other as if to say, 'This wasn't in the programme.'

'As you may well have noticed, a brand-new stadium is being built in Brentford. This stadium is to be officially opened early next year.

 132

However, the field and many of the facilities are already in place and the West London Youth Sports Association are organising a special summer camp for children who have shown outstanding talent in our community. I am one of the sponsors and I will be running some of the training sessions there this summer. *Running*? Heh, heh. You get it?'

People laughed a bit. I got it. I know what puns are.

'We are right now scouting for gifted young athletes to take part in this summer camp, and today, I noticed a boy on the track with exceptional running talent ... and that boy is ...'

I saw Mitch puff up his chest and smile to himself smugly.

Of course, it had to be Mitch, didn't it?

Jimmy sat bolt upright and looked from left to right. 'Wait. What?' he said.

Then everyone started cheering.

'Jimmy, it's you!' I said.

'I would like to invite Jimmy from Year Five to come up here, please,' said Yu Kerubo. There wasn't a medal or a certificate or anything, because I think Yu Kerubo had only just decided to offer Jimmy the scholarship to the summer camp, but it didn't matter. I'd never seen Jimmy look so happy. He bounced up from the ground and dashed through the crowds.

Everyone was patting him on the back again. And this time for a much better reason.

And there he was. Standing in front of the whole school, shaking Yu Kerubo's hand. Everyone was cheering and clapping and Yiayia was shouting, 'Bravo Jimmy, bravo!' Mum and Dad both had tears in their eyes.

And me, I stood up and clapped the hardest. For my twin Jimmy. The winner!

Mum had got me and Jimmy new clothes and matching suitcases because we were flying somewhere hot and sunny with blue, blue sea for our holiday. We were going to Cyprus!

The two of us were especially excited because we'd never been to Cyprus before. We'd never even been out of England. When Mum and Dad were together, we would go on holiday to places like Norfolk or the Lake District or Scotland, which Yiayia could never understand.

'Why go where is always rain?' she'd say.

'Why no go stay with all you aunties, you uncles, you cousins in Cyprus?'

I think that was one of the main reasons we didn't go. Dad was from such a small family that our mega-sized Greek one was a bit too much for him. He said that if we went to Cyprus, it wouldn't be much like a holiday, we'd be too tied down having to visit everyone's brother-in-law's great-uncle's fifth cousins.

We have separate holidays with Dad now. He can take us to Cornwall or Wales when it's his turn. But this year we were going to Cyprus with Mum and Yiayia, and Yiayia couldn't be more pleased. I think she misses her family out there a lot, because when she came to London, a hundred million years ago, she came on her own and got married here and everything. Her brother, my Bapou Nikos, stayed behind. He's too old to travel now so Yiayia doesn't get to see him so much. He lives with his daughter, my Auntie Maria, she's my mum's cousin, and my Uncle Costas, and then they have two kids, Elena and Michael, which makes them my second cousins – I know, complicated family, right? Anyway, that's who we'd be staying with.

I thought I was going to enjoy being on an aeroplane, but the journey was a nightmare because I was travel sick the whole way. Mum had to keep holding paper bags over my face and it didn't help that Jimmy kept shaming me by letting the entire plane know about it.

'Urrgh, Cally's spewing again!' He might as well have got the air stewards to announce it over the loudspeaker.

He also fidgeted with absolutely anything he could find – opening and closing the little fold-up tray,

flicking the seat belt buckle up and down,

shuffling through all the magazines,

getting up about fifty-billion times to go to the toilet – so he could muck about with all the mini compartments in there as well, no doubt.

And whenever the trolley went past, he'd pester Mum to buy him something off it.

'Will you just give us a break, Jimmy?' I groaned. 'You're making me feel even more sick.'

Poor Mum, between mopping up my puke and trying to keep Jimmy in his seat, I think she found the plane ride really hard. 'I'm beginning to think your dad had the right idea, sticking with good old Cornwall,' she said. That was one of the first times she'd said something positive about Dad in a long time. It was the only good thing about that plane journey.

Yiayia slept through all of it, with her seat tilted back and her mouth open, as if she was catching flies.

At one point she snored a bit loudly and woke herself up. She looked around all surprised for a moment, then went back to sleep again.

It was such a relief when we landed. Stepping off onto the metal staircase, I felt a rush of warm air hit my face. I breathed it in, the smell of a different country. Dawn was just breaking and the giant orange sun was rising in the sky.

'Wow!' said Jimmy. 'How come everything's shimmering, Mum?'

'That's the heat. And it's only first thing in the morning. Just you wait till it gets to the middle of the day. Forty degrees, you know.'

Auntie Maria and Uncle Costas were waiting for us, smiling through the glass wall that divided the arrivals room from the way out.

'There they are! Ya-soo! Ya-soo!' said Yiayia, waving her arms off. She was wide awake now.

We had to wait for our suitcases by this big conveyor belt thing that spiralled round the arrivals room.

'Do they come out through that little flappy door over there?' I asked.

'I hope so,' said Yiayia.

Just then, the belt began to move, snaking round the room.

'Cool!' cried Jimmy. And before anyone could stop him, he'd jumped onto it and was riding it like a surfboard.

'What are you doing, Jimmy! Get off there! Now!' yelled Mum.

A red light started flashing on a pole in the middle of the machine and a siren blared.

Jimmy lost his balance and landed on his bottom. 'I can't . . .' he panicked.

Worse still, Jimmy was heading for one of the flappy doors. It was going to swallow him up. Where did it lead to?

'Heeeelp! Heeeelp!' shouted Jimmy.

 146

'Heeeelp! Heeeelp!'

Yiayia was throwing her arms up in the air, crying, 'Mana mou! Mana mou!'

Luckily, a big man at the end of the carousel yanked Jimmy up by the belt of his shorts and lifted him off. We all went rushing over. Mum clipped Jimmy round the ear. 'You silly, silly boy! What on earth were you thinking?'

That's Jimmy's problem. He doesn't think.

Everyone stared at us. *So* embarrassing. The security guard was giving us angry looks.

Mum tried to apologise but he just shook his head. Luckily the suitcases started to come out then and everyone focused on looking for their bags, but I was still dying inside.

Finally, we got all our luggage together, showed the angry security man our passports and then we were free to get started on our holiday. We went through the automatic doors, into the arms of Auntie Maria and Uncle Costas. There were many kisses all round, with everyone bumping into one another, not sure who to kiss next or who hadn't kissed who yet.

I think Auntie Maria got to me at least three times. Jimmy wiped the kisses off when people weren't looking.

We had to split up into two cars because of all the suitcases. Uncle Costas went with the luggage in one car and the rest of us went with Auntie Maria. We left Larnaca Airport and headed for Deftera, a small village outside the capital city, Nicosia, where Yiayia had grown up. I wound the window right down to get that amazing warm air on my face again. Everything was hazy, dusty, rugged and open. The land was hilly and dry.

'Bit like a desert, isn't it?' said Jimmy.

'This just motorway,' Yiayia explained. 'Many flower and tree in village. Is beautiful.'

Yiayia was right. As we got closer to Auntie Maria's house, the sweetest smell, like perfume, drifted in through the car windows.

'Mmmm! That's the jasmine,' said Mum, closing her eyes and taking in a deep breath.

'Will Elena and Michael be there?' I asked. We'd had loads of fun together with our second cousins when they came to stay with us in London the year before.

'Yes, they're dying to see you. They're waiting to have their breakfast with you.'

'Brilliant,' shouted Jimmy. 'Then can we play football?'

'OK, but I'm putting you both to bed this afternoon,' said Mum. 'It's been a long journey.'

'No way!' said Jimmy. 'I don't want to go to bed!'

'You'd better get used to it. Everyone sleeps in the afternoons here. It gets too hot to do anything else. Siesta, they call it,' said Mum.

'I'm not sleeping in the daytime!' protested Jimmy.

'You'll have to. Everyone else does,' said Mum.

'How boring is that?!'

Auntie Maria parked up on the dusty drive.

 150

'Come on. Let's go inside. We'll have some soup and then you can get some rest.'

'Soup *now*?'

Everything's the wrong way round in Cyprus. Soup for breakfast. Sleeps in the daytime. I'm glad most people speak English, at least. I get shy when I have to speak Greek, even though Mum makes us go to Greek School to learn it.

'Wow! Look at that tree. It's got real-life lemons growing off it!' said Jimmy.

'Yes, and some of them are in the avgolemoni soupa I've made you. So let's get in now and have some,' said Auntie Maria.

★

It was brilliant seeing Elena and Michael again. Michael's a bit younger than me and Jimmy, and he's always laughing – I've never seen someone who laughs so much in my whole life. It makes you want to laugh too when you're around him. Elena's almost a teenager and

 151

she's very pretty but she thinks it's really cool that we come from London and is always asking us about it and whether we know any famous people. Jimmy told her about Yu Kerubo but I think she wanted to know about popstars or actors or something, not old athletes.

The best thing about Elena and Michael's house was all the animals. They'd got chickens in the yard and Jimmy loved chasing them about, flapping his arms as if he was a chicken too. I kept telling him it was cruel and to stop it, but Elena and Michael thought it was hilarious for some unknown reason. I could almost understand why Michael might think Jimmy's funny. He thinks everything's funny. But I was disappointed that Elena was joining in with all that nonsense.

She's nearly thirteen. I had hoped we might hang out together more, just us – she's amazing at gymnastics and when she came to England last year she started teaching me how to do backward walkovers and stuff. I thought we might do more of that, maybe make up routines together. But she seemed to prefer clowning around in the yard with the boys.

As well as the chickens, sometimes the goats that lived up on the hill would come randomly wandering into the yard and then Jimmy went *really* daft. He'd start acting like they were wild beasts coming to get him. Really they just wanted to have a bit of a munch on the shrubs and flowers and they were about as interested in Jimmy's annoyingness as I was. I thought the goats were cool and they even let me stroke them, until Bapou Nikos got up and started waving his walking stick at them shouting, 'Fiye! Fiye!' which is Greek for 'Buzz off!', I think.

 153

We also got to see lots of donkeys. People keep them as pets in Cyprus. Mostly the old people. I think it's for helping them to carry things – like living shopping trolleys. Elena and Michael don't have a donkey, but they do have a dog, Hari. He's so cute. He's got golden shaggy fur, floppy ears and big soppy eyes. But we didn't get to play with him that much because mostly he's kept tied up at the back of the house. He sleeps outside as well, in a kennel. I thought that was a bit sad, but apparently it's normal for dogs in Cyprus. Me and Jimmy went over to stroke him a lot every day, and he always jumped up and started wagging his tail when he saw us. Auntie Maria let us take him all the leftover bones from dinner too. So Hari soon became our best friend ever.

As well as all the animals, there are masses of minibeasts in Cyprus. You can hear the cicadas singing in the trees all day long. Jimmy didn't know what cicadas were, so I had to explain to him that they're like crickets or giant grasshoppers. Bapou Nikos told us they call them 'tsitsikas' – what a cool word – it's like the sound they make when they rub their legs together as if playing a very scratchy violin or something.

And every five minutes I could also hear Jimmy calling, 'Look! Look, Cally! It's a lizard! A lizard!'

But whenever I rushed over to see, they'd zip away and hide in the bushes. They got too scared. We had to be quieter around them, but try telling that to Jimmy.

One time, when I was crouching down by the rock garden to see if I could get a glimpse of one, something tickled the back of my neck.

155

'Aargh, Cally, it's a giant beetle!' cried Jimmy.

'What? Where? Get it off me! Get it off me!' I screamed, doing a crazy flappy dance with my arms and legs.

And then I heard the others laughing. I stopped and turned to see my cousins rolling about all over the place in hysterics and Jimmy waving a long piece of grass in the air.

'Like my beetle?' he grinned.

'Ha, ha, Calista. You should see your face,' wheezed Michael, clutching his belly as if

Jimmy's trick was the funniest thing ever.

And I didn't like it when Elena started doing an impression of me, dancing around the yard squealing, 'Get it away! Get it away! Get it away!'

Ganging up on me. That wasn't very nice. And it might have been just a piece of grass that time, but it's not as if there aren't the most gigantic creepy-crawlies for real everywhere in Cyprus. So I think that was just plain mean of Jimmy.

But Jimmy's fake beetle was nothing compared to what was waiting for us in Bapou Nikos' bathroom later that afternoon.

Bapou Nikos lives in a side-building next to Auntie Maria's and Uncle Costas's house. It's an ancient mud hut from the olden days. It's next to the chicken shed and might as well be a chicken shed too, if you ask me. The family have offered to build him a more modern house, but he likes it that way. It's where he's lived ever since he was a boy.

When we were out playing in the yard, we would use his bathroom if we wanted to go to the toilet. I was scared of that bathroom. A trillion creepy-crawlies lived in the cracks and dark corners. So I always went as quickly as I could. I didn't want to get ants in my pants. They're big fat red ones in Cyprus, too. Elena says they're that colour because they suck your blood.

But what was lurking in the bathroom that

day was no red ant. It was when
I went to wash my hands
that I saw it. There by the
plughole, was a gigantic
scorpion, with a rust-
brown shell, thick like
armour and huge pincers. Its
tail was curling up and down in slow motion.

I screamed my head off. Mum and Jimmy
came running. The others weren't around.
Elena and Michael had gone to the supermarket
with their mum and dad, and Yiayia and Bapou
Nikos were having an extra-long afternoon nap.

We stood together, staring at the creature.

'Oh . . . my . . . God,' said Jimmy.

It was the scariest thing ever. It didn't
matter that the slippery sides of the sink had
it trapped.

'Kill it! Kill it, Mum!' I cried.

Mum turned on the taps.

'Yeah that's it,' cheered Jimmy. 'Drown it!'

Probably not the kindest thing. But that scorpion was evil.

'Can scorpions jump?'

'Are they poisonous?'

'Do their tails really sting?'

'Turn the taps on more, Mum! Make the water come out faster!'

'That's as much as they will go,' said Mum.

Then the strangest thing happened. As the water surrounded the scorpion, it swelled and doubled in size, right there in front of us. Everybody screamed then. Even Mum.

Bapou Nikos appeared in the doorway, all bent over his walking stick. 'What is problem?' he said. He shuffled over to the sink, and noticing the scorpion, just said, 'Ama . . .' then poked it.

The scorpion sprang into action, rushing about the basin in circles.

We screamed again.

That brought Yiayia scurrying over too.

She took one look at the scorpion, marched outside, grabbed two sticks from the woodpile and returned to the bathroom as if ready for battle. She gripped the scorpion between the two pieces of wood. She raised it high in the air. Its tail curled up and down, its pincers thrashed about. Me and Jimmy ducked, shielding our heads with our arms, screaming the whole time. Yiayia carried the scorpion out to the yard and lobbed it over the back fence, far, far away into the field beyond. She stuck the sticks back into the pile, slapped her palms together and said, 'That's it. Finish now, scorpion.'

★

The house in Deftera is not that near the coast, so you have to go by car if you want to get to the seaside. So we were really excited when the time came for us to go on a day trip to Cape Greco. Uncle Costas keeps a fishing boat out there so that's where the family most likes to go.

 162

'Pleeeeeease can we take Hari with us? Pleeeeeease.' Jimmy had been begging for us to bring the dog along to the beach all morning. 'We can't leave him behind, he's going to feel all left out. It's not fair.'

Hari flopped to the ground and looked up with extra-sad puppy-dog eyes. It was as if he and Jimmy were some sort of double act. Jimmy does that when he's trying to get his own way too.

'OK, OK,' sighed Auntie Maria. 'But we keep him on his lead all the time.'

'Hoooooooraaay!' cheered Jimmy, punching the air. He'd already learned how to win everyone over in Cyprus too. Or wear them down, more like.

We packed up the cars with everyone and everything – a massive picnic, beach mats, umbrella shades, bats and balls and even a stack of chairs tied to the roof-rack.

Jimmy's endless chanting of, 'Are we nearly

163

there yet? Are we nearly there yet?' finally changed to, 'The sea! I can see the sea!' as the car drove over the top of a hill and down to Cape Greco bay.

It was totally *wow*. The sea was bright turquoise and it sparkled like magic. The sand was gold and the beach itself was like one of those pirate coves with trees all around and what looked like secret caves beyond the rocks. I couldn't wait to be in the middle of it all. Neither could Jimmy, who had absolutely no patience when it came to unloading the cars and setting up our spot on the beach.

'Can I go now? Can I go now?' Jimmy was running on the spot, digging a hole in the sand with his feet. Hari copied him and started digging too.

'Let's at least get some sun cream on you, Jimmy,' said Mum.

When at last we were free to play, Jimmy raced into the sea crying, 'Geronimoooo!'

I followed with our cousins. The sea was warm, like a bath. And the water was so clear, you could see shoals of tiny little silver fishes swimming about.

Mum, Auntie Maria and Yiayia stayed back with Hari, relaxing in the shade under the big umbrellas, and Uncle Costas went out in his fishing boat. He promised us that he'd take us out in it later too.

 165

We had a great time, playing in the sea and on the beach, burying each other in the sand, turning Jimmy into a mermaid sculpture and digging holes so deep the water would come up at the bottom.

After lunch, Jimmy looked around him, wondering what to do next. Hari gazed up at Jimmy, woofed and started wagging his tail.

'Can I take Hari for a walk? Pleeeeeease. Just a little walk.'

Hari wagged his tail faster and woofed again.

Auntie Maria looked at Mum.

'Well, I don't think we'll get a minute's peace until we say yes,' Mum said.

'But only if you go with Cally and your cousins,' said Auntie Maria.

'But we were going to go back in the sea with the inflatables,' I said. Jimmy had persuaded Yiayia to buy us a giant orca whale, which we'd called Orinoco, and I'd chosen a rubber ring that was like a pink flamingo and we'd named Fenella. Yiayia thought they were a bit expensive, but she caved in as usual. 'But thirty euro just for balloon?' she'd said, shaking her head.

Jimmy began to do his whinging act. 'I want to take Hari for a walk, now!'

Yiayia, who could see one of his meltdowns coming from a mile off, said, 'Maybe first take dog, then play with balloon.'

Michael picked up Orinoco and started heading for the sea anyway.

'Hey, Michael! Wait for me!' shouted Elena, grabbing Fenella and running after her brother.

'But I wanna take Hari for a walk . . .' Jimmy's lip began to wobble.

'Fine,' I said. 'I'll go with Jimmy.'

Jimmy always gets his own way.

I didn't mind too much though, cos I love Hari as well. I really want a dog, but we're not allowed one at home because Mum says they're too much responsibility. I want Dad to get one, so he won't be lonely, but his flat's too small and he's always out at work so he says it's not practical.

'Can I at least hold his lead?' I said. We'd been given strict instructions to keep Hari under control, especially on the beach, because he gets excited with crowds and he's such a greedy thing, he'd have his nose in everyone's picnics.

'I'll hold his lead on the way and you can have it on the way back,' said Jimmy. I felt too hot to argue so Jimmy got his way as usual.

We headed towards the caves at the end of the beach. It became quite rocky as we got nearer, and the sea was not so calm there. The waves crashed against the rocks, spraying up high in the air.

'I think we should turn back now,' I said.

'Why do you always have to be such a scaredy cat, Cally?' said Jimmy.

'It's better than being an idiot like you. Always getting us into trouble.'

'Who you calling an idiot?' said Jimmy, making a fist.

'You!'

It was Hari who settled the argument, because at that moment he started barking at a seagull and pulling on his lead.

'Hari! Hari! Stop!' cried Jimmy.

But Hari tugged the lead so hard, that Jimmy couldn't keep hold of it. Hari ripped away from Jimmy and bounded over the rocks and into the cave.

'Now look what you've done,' I said.

'Me? It wasn't *my* fault!'

'You're the one who wouldn't let me hold his lead . . .'

But Jimmy was already leaping over the rocks and chasing after Hari.

'Wait . . . Jimmy . . . No . . .'

Jimmy disappeared into the cave with Hari, and I had no choice but to follow.

I don't know how Hari and Jimmy had got over those rocks so quickly, because I found it quite a struggle. It was really slippy and the waves kept splashing over me, practically knocking me over. And I could swear the sea was getting higher all the time.

I was relieved when I managed to get over

170

the worst of the rocks and reached the entrance to the cave. The ground was smoother there and it even became sandy as you went in.

I found Jimmy crouched down by the cave wall, shivering. Hari was nuzzled up next to him and licking Jimmy's leg. That's when I saw it. Blood.

'I think I'm hurt,' said Jimmy.

That was an understatement. He'd got a massive cut on his leg from the rocks.

'Jimmy!'

'It's OK. I'll be all right.'

'I said we shouldn't have come.'

'Yeah . . . well . . . you always have to be right, don't ya?' said Jimmy.

'And you always have to be so wrong!'

But there wasn't really any time for arguing. The tide looked like it was coming in fast. It had almost covered the rocks now and was tearing at the opening to the cave too.

'Take off your T-shirt, Jimmy. I'll wrap it round your leg to stop the bleeding,' I said.

When we'd done that, I looked up and saw that the sea had now reached right up to where we were sitting.

'How we gonna get out of here?' asked Jimmy.

'I don't know,' I said, feeling a lot more scared than I sounded. We are both quite good swimmers, but there was no way we could risk trying to get through that. The sea was too choppy and there were all those rocks. We'd be ripped to shreds.

Hari started barking and running round in circles.

'We'll send Hari for help,' I said. I took Hari by the collar and looked seriously into his eyes.

'Now, Hari. You need to be a really good boy and go and find Auntie Maria. Show her where we are.'

'How's he supposed to understand you? He only speaks Greek.'

'He doesn't speak anything, you fool. He speaks dog language. Anyway, dogs are clever. He understands.' I looked back into Hari's eyes, 'You understand, don't you, Hari mou?'

Hari woofed, turned on his heels and went bounding out into the sea.

'Go on, Hari!' cried Jimmy. Then he said, 'Haddeh, Hari. Haddeh!' which is 'Go on, Hari,' in Greek, just in case.

We watched him swim away, the waves splashing over him. He even disappeared under them, but then his golden head would bob back up again. We lost sight of him completely as he rounded the rocks and went in the direction of the main beach. I prayed he'd make it.

We went to sit down at the back of the cave where there was a ledge in the rocky wall a bit higher up, and watched the sea closing in.

'Do you think Hari will do it?' asked Jimmy.

'He has to. He's our only hope,' I said, gazing out to sea.

Jimmy started jabbering on, saying annoying things like, 'What happens when the sea swallows you up?' and, 'Is it true your whole life flashes before your eyes when you're drowning, Cally?' until I couldn't take it any more and I yelled at him to shut up and stop being so dumb.

But that only made things worse because then Jimmy's bottom lip began to wobble which meant only one thing – he was going to cry. And he did. But not in his usual tantrumy meltdown way. He just hung his head and started to cry quietly.

Maybe I shouldn't have shouted at him.

 175

I put my hand on his shoulder and said, 'I'm sorry, Jimmy. How's your hurt leg doing? Shall we have a look?' And I gently peeled away the T-shirt bandage. The cut was going all purple around the edges. What if it went septic or something? But I didn't want Jimmy to be scared so I tried to focus on the positives – that's what Dad says we should do whenever we're feeling bad. So I said, 'It's stopped bleeding, at least.' And then I carefully rebandaged his leg.

We sat there for what seemed like for ever, watching the sea flooding in and willing it not to come too close.

'I'm sorry too, Cally,' said Jimmy. 'I should have let you hold Hari. We'd never have got into this mess if I'd given you a turn.'

'It's OK, Jimmy,' I said. 'It wasn't your fault.' Even though it kind of was, but there was no point making him feel worse. Things were bad enough already.

Every now and then, Jimmy expressed

another one of his fears. But I let him. 'What if Mum never finds out what happened to us?' he said. Then a few seconds later, 'I bet Yiayia will be getting really worried,' and then, 'I don't want Yiayia to be worried,' and then, 'I want Mum . . .'

I knew what he meant, but I'm the oldest, by seventeen minutes and forty-two seconds, so I just had to be brave and put my arm round him.

And all the time, the sea was coming in, closer and closer.

And then we heard it.

Woof! Woof! Woof!

It had to be . . .

We sprang to our feet.

'Oh my goodness!'

'It's Hari to the rescue!' cheered Jimmy.

We clutched onto each other and jumped up and down in celebration, because suddenly Uncle Costas' fishing boat came into view, with Hari at the bow, barking his head off.

Uncle Costas steered the boat as close as he could to the cave and dropped the anchor.

He grabbed two life jackets then climbed overboard and swam up to us. The waves churned at the mouth of the cave, but he fought through them until he reached us inside.

We rushed over to him and he scooped us up in his big strong arms.

'Is OK now. Everybody safe now. Is OK.'

Uncle Costas had to take us one at a time back to the boat. Jimmy went first cos he was the most scared and he'd started shivering really badly. Uncle Costas got Jimmy to put his arms round his neck and he swam off with him on his back. I watched on nervously as they reached the boat. Hari was barking like crazy the whole time.

Then Uncle Costas came back for me and we battled through the water together. I held onto him as tight as I could but it wasn't easy. The waves were nasty and I kept swallowing gulps of salty water, which made me feel really sick. But we got there in the end and once we had heaved ourselves back onto the boat, Hari at last stopped barking and started panting happily and wagging his tail.

'Good boy, Hari, good boy,' I said, burying my head in his neck.

Uncle Costas steered us back to shore. I don't think a pirate cave rescue was quite what he had in mind when he'd promised us a boat ride earlier on that day, but nothing's ever straightforward when Jimmy's involved.

We got quite a telling off from Auntie Maria, Mum and Yiayia when we got back. They were nowhere near as soft on us as Uncle Costas had been. Elena and Michael couldn't believe what we'd done. I wasn't sure if they were shocked or impressed, but they both stood there gawping at us with expressions on their faces that said,

'You're in BIG trouble!'

But that was my twin Jimmy all over. Always getting in trouble and always dragging me into it as well. And that's why he's the most-annoying-brother-in-the-whole-wide-world.

★

But the rest of our amazing holiday in Cyprus more than made up for it. And when it was over and it was time to fly back to England, I stood at the top of the metal staircase just before getting on the plane and took one last look back at the shimmering land. I breathed in the sweet warm air and turned to go, knowing I'd be taking so much of Cyprus home with me in my heart . . . the warmth and amazing aromas of Auntie Maria's house . . . the mucking around with Elena and Michael in their yard with all the animals – it had been such a laugh. I have to admit, I even secretly thought Jimmy's chicken impression was quite funny. And I'd miss the goats too. But not the creepy-crawlies, and definitely not the scorpion – the way Bapou Nikos just poked it with a stick, and the way Yiayia catapulted it over into the next field! But the thing both me and Jimmy would probably remember the most was the day we had to be saved from the sea-flooded cave, with Hari the hero to our rescue. Yes, it had been quite a trip . . .

'Come on, Cally,' yelled Jimmy, dragging me back to reality and onto the plane. 'What you waiting for? It's time to go.'

'All right, all right. Keep your hair on. I'm coming.'

'Hope you don't puke your guts out all the way home as well,' jeered Jimmy.

'Hope you don't annoy every single person on the entire plane with your mega annoyingness.'

'Yiayiaaaaaaa! Muuuuuuuuuum! Tell her. Cally's being mean to me,' wailed Jimmy.

'You're both as bad as each other,' Mum sighed.

She's always saying that. Probably because we're twins. It's not true, of course. But that's the way it will always be. Cos me and Jimmy . . . well, we'll always be a pair, won't we? And somehow that's OK.

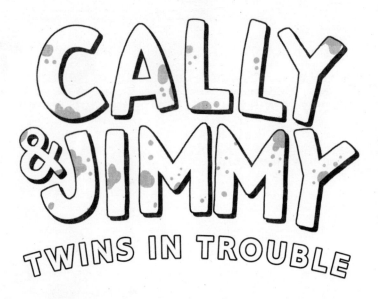

CALLY & JIMMY

TWINS IN TROUBLE

ZOE ANTONIADES

ILLUSTRATED BY **KATIE KEAR**

It's double trouble when Cally and Jimmy are around.

Another four fantastic
stories about everyone's
favourite twins!

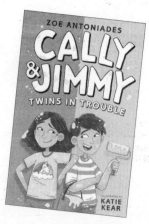